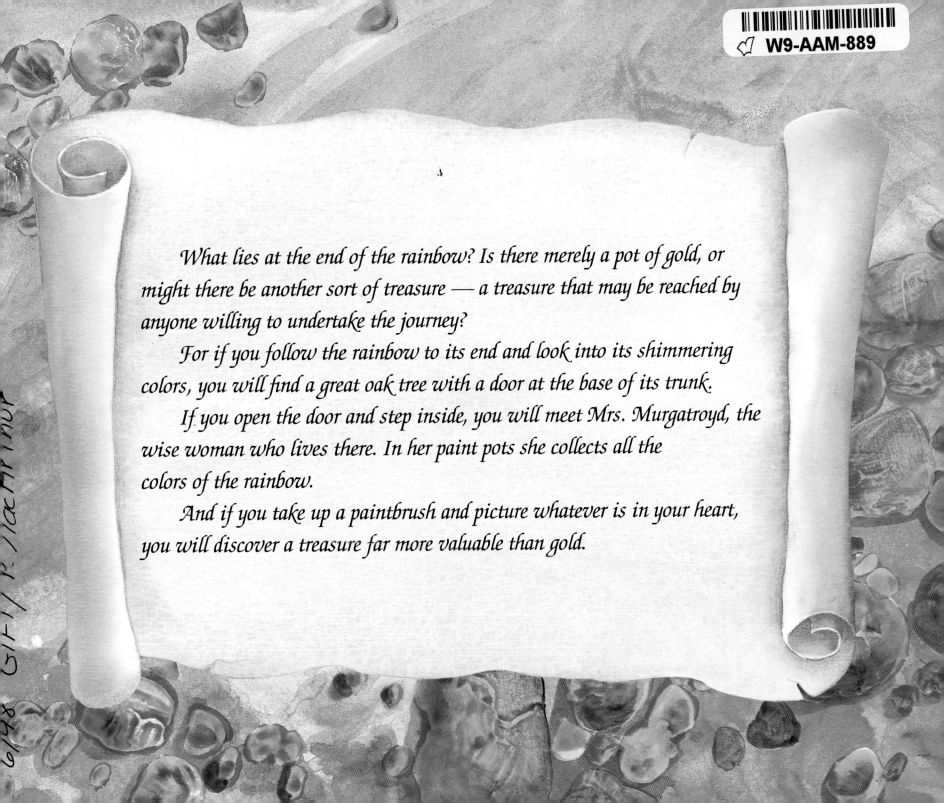

What lies at the end of the rainbow? Is there merely a pot of gold, or might there be another sort of treasure — a treasure that may be reached by anyone willing to undertake the journey?

For if you follow the rainbow to its end and look into its shimmering colors, you will find a great oak tree with a door at the base of its trunk.

If you open the door and step inside, you will meet Mrs. Murgatroyd, the wise woman who lives there. In her paint pots she collects all the colors of the rainbow.

And if you take up a paintbrush and picture whatever is in your heart, you will discover a treasure far more valuable than gold.

Red Poppies for a Little Bird

Enchanté books are dedicated to the children who inspired them

Series concept by Ayman Sawaf and Kevin Ryerson
Developed by Liz Farrington from true stories
Copyright © 1993 by Enchanté Publishing
MRS. MURGATROYD Character copyright ©1993 by Enchanté
MRS. MURGATROYD is a trademark of Enchanté
Series format and design by Jaclyne Scardova

Enchanté Publishing,
180 Harbor Drive, Sausalito, CA 94965

Printed in Hong Kong

Library of Congress Cataloging-in-Publication Data
Farrington, Liz
Red poppies for a little bird/ story created by Liz Farrington; written by Jonathan Sherwood;
illustrated by Brian McGovern. — 1st ed.
     p.   cm.
Summary: Magic paints help Tom to face the secret guilt that makes him get into trouble at
school and at home.
ISBN 1-56844-005-7
[1. Death – Fiction.   2. Guilt – Fiction.   3. Dogs – Fiction.]   I. Sherwood, Jon.
II. McGovern, Brian, ill.   III. Title.
PZ7.F24618Re   1993   [E] — dc20   93-19259

First Edition
10 9 8 7 6 5 4 3 2 1

Red Poppies for a Little Bird

Story created by Liz Farrington
Written by Jonathan Sherwood
Illustrated by Brian McGovern

Enchanté Publishing

Ms. Tuttle shook her head and handed him his report. "I'm very disappointed in you, Tom. We both know you could do so much better."

Tom looked at the red *F* in the top margin and scowled. He crumpled the report and tossed it into a wastepaper basket. "Two points!" he said, but no one cheered.

"No points," Ms. Tuttle said and continued handing out reports.

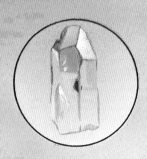

At the soccer game after school, Tom let every ball kicked his way just roll by.

"What's with you, Tom?" said Mr. Forbes. "Early in the season you kicked more goals than all the rest of the team put together. Now — nothing. If you've got a problem, say so."

Tom shrugged and stared at his shoes.

"Okay. If you can't talk and you can't play, you're out of here," he said with a jerk of his thumb. "Come back when you're ready to play!"

Coach Forbes blew his whistle, and Tom's teammates scrambled back to their positions as Tom shuffled off the field.

"I want you to start your homework before you do anything else," Tom's mother said when he got home. "I got another call from Ms. Tuttle. You've gone from mostly *A*'s to *F*'s in all your classes. I don't understand it, Tom. You've always been such a good student, and now you're failing. Is something bothering you? What's wrong?"

"Nothing," Tom said angrily, and slammed the door to his room.

When his dad checked in on him, Tom was lying on his back, staring at the ceiling.

"Tom! I thought you were supposed to be doing your homework. And your room's a mess. I told you a week ago to clean it up!"

"I *know!*" Tom shouted.

"You *'know'* but you're not doing it. Do you think I'm going to do your homework and clean your room for you? Now do it! And when you're done, wash Buster. You wanted that old dog. He's your responsibility." Tom's dad shut the door.

Tom waited till he heard his dad's footsteps fade. Then he opened his window, climbed out, and dropped to the ground.

It was hot and the still air seemed almost too heavy to breathe. As he'd done the day before, and the day before that, Tom trudged toward the woods. He loved hiking. For years he'd been doing it with his parents, and Buster, too. But now he went alone, without even telling his mom or dad. He knew it worried them, but that didn't stop him. It didn't seem to matter any more than his schoolwork or soccer or his dog. Tom just felt numb.

Tom had arrived at the old rock quarry. He picked up a flat rock and threw it with all his might. It skimmed down toward the bottom of the quarry and shattered into a thousand pieces.

What good is anything? Tom thought. He'd tried extra hard to be good, but he just couldn't keep it up. Now he was failing school, he'd let his teammates down, and his parents were always mad at him. Tom felt a sharp pain in his arm and looked down. He had jabbed himself with a sharp stone and his arm was bleeding.

Oh no! he thought. *What'll I tell Mom and Dad this time?* He couldn't say that he fell and cut his arm. That's what he'd told them last time he'd done it. *Why do I keep hurting myself?*

Tom's arm hurt, but not as much as he hurt inside.

A bird settled on a nearby tree and started to sing. Tom couldn't stand it. He jumped up and raced down the hill until he came to a clear mountain stream, then plunged his injured arm into the icy water. Drops of bright red blood dripped and mingled with an array of different colors in the fast-moving stream. But where were the other colors coming from?

Tom looked up. A woman was rinsing paint pots and brushes in the stream. Beyond her a rainbow seemed to be pouring its colors into a great oak tree — a tree with a door standing open in the trunk!

The woman smiled at him, then stood up and stepped quietly into the tree, bearing her pots and brushes. Her smile was an invitation, and Tom followed.

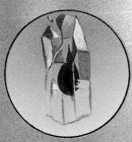

Inside the hollow tree, the glow of the rainbow lit up the room. His mind racing, Tom's eyes were drawn to a shelf where the rainbow flowed into several small pots and turned into paint, one color for each pot. As he gazed, enchanted, at the shimmering colors working their magic, Tom began to feel calmer. And when the woman said, "I'm glad you've come, Tom. I'm Mrs. Murgatroyd," he felt at ease.

She had placed a sheet of white paper on a table. Tom sat down and lifted a brush. He
enjoyed painting, but it seemed that no matter what he started out with, he always ended up
painting a picture of his dog, Buster. He rubbed his arm and blood dripped onto the blank
paper. Not wanting Mrs. Murgatroyd to see his wound, he quickly unrolled his shirt sleeve and
covered it up.

Hoping Mrs. Murgatroyd would think that the blood was paint, Tom dipped his brush into a pot of red and began painting. He worked quickly, as if the paint were flowing out of him.

Soon a fierce-looking Buster stood in his picture. And there in his mouth was a tattered bundle of bloody feathers, a tiny bird caught in Buster's jaws. Tom had never, ever, painted Buster this way — not with the bird in his mouth!

It was an awful picture. Tom grabbed the paper, crumpled it into a tight ball, and threw it out the door. The paint was still wet, and his hands were covered in red. Tom glanced at Mrs. Murgatroyd and stumbled outside into the woods.

Tom suddenly found himself whisked back two years into the past. Frozen, he watched himself at age seven, walking through the woods with Buster. He saw the little bird chirping and flopping about on the path in front of them, dragging one wing along the ground. He saw Buster stop, cock his head at the bird, and charge. Tom saw his younger self shout, "No! Stop, Buster! Stop!" then chase after the dog. But Buster snapped up the floundering bird before Little Tom could grab him. "Drop it, Buster! Drop it!" The younger Tom lunged at Buster, but each time he got close, Buster raced away, thinking it was just a game.

Finally, Little Tom grabbed Buster's collar, pried open his jaws, and took the tiny scrap from his mouth. The bird shivered.

"No! Don't die!" Little Tom was frantic. "What should I do? I don't know what to do!"

The bird grew still. It was too late.

"Why did you have to go and die?" Little Tom shouted. "You didn't have to let Buster catch you, you stupid bird! Why didn't you hide someplace?"

Little Tom stood there, staring down at the bloody bundle of feathers. Then he put the dead bird down and began to dig in the soil.

At last Big Tom could speak. "Tom, wait!"

Little Tom stopped and looked up at his older self.

"We've got to talk," said Big Tom.

The two boys sat at the foot of an oak tree. As Big Tom listened,
Little Tom poured out all his guilty feelings.

"It's my fault," he said. "I should have trained Buster better — he
would have stopped when I told him to. He would have dropped the bird if I'd trained him
right. I can't believe I just let it die! I should have run to the vet's or something. What will
Mom and Dad say? I can't tell them. I can't tell anybody. What I'll have to do is be extra
good to make up for it. I'll make straight *A*'s in school and kick more goals than anybody
else in soccer. Yes! *I will I will I will!*"

When Little Tom had finished, Big Tom stood up and said, "Come with me." He picked
up the bird, took Little Tom by the hand, and set off through the woods. Buster followed at
their heels.

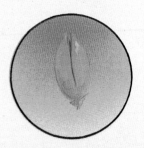

Together, the boys did what Little Tom said he should have done. They ran with the small bird all the way to the vet's office.

Cupping the bird in his hand, the vet adjusted his glasses and shook his head. "There's nothing you could have done to save this bird," he said. "And there's nothing I could have done, either."

The boys raced back home, yelling for their parents. Their mom ran from the garden, their dad from the house. They looked at the bird and sighed.

"There's nothing we could have done," Mom said.

"It was too badly hurt to live," added Dad. "I'm sorry."

When they were back at the tree in the forest, Big Tom said, "You couldn't have saved the bird no matter what you did."

"It's still my fault," said Little Tom. "I should have trained Buster better."

"It wasn't your fault. By the time you got Buster, he was too old to train," said Big Tom, rubbing the dog's ears. "It's hard to train an old dog, isn't it, Buster?"

Together, Big and Little Tom buried the small bundle of feathers. They hugged each other and gazed down at the tiny grave.

"It couldn't be saved," Big Tom said.

"I know," said Little Tom.

Suddenly an acorn bounced off his head. Startled, Tom looked around. He was kneeling beside the little bird's grave. And there on the mound bloomed brilliant, orange-red poppies!

All of a sudden, he wanted to tell somebody what had happened. About Buster and the little bird and trying to be extra good and then giving up. *All* of it!

I'll tell my folks, he thought. *I'll tell them first.*

Just then Buster came bounding through the trees.

"Buster! C'mere, Buster. Hi, old fella. Good boy." Tom rubbed Buster's ears, then grabbed him in a big hug. "Sorry I haven't taken you hiking like we used to. But from now on, Buster, whenever I go, you can come with me."

While Tom washed his hands in the stream, Buster jumped in and splashed and shook off, a sudden rainbow catching the spray in a beam of sunlight.

And with Buster sniffing along behind him, Tom walked back through the woods toward home, whistling like a bird.

Station Avenue

Elementary School

South Yarmouth, MA 02664

31276000032093